Ivy Loves to Give

FREYA BLACKWOOD

ARTHUR A. LEVINE BOOKS
An Imprint of Scholastic Inc.

Ivy loves to give.

Sometimes her presents
are the wrong size,

don't fit properly,

taste funny,

or feel strange.

But other times,
her presents feel good,

taste delicious,

fit perfectly,

and are exactly the right size.

Ivy loves to give,

but sometimes she
would rather keep.

So when someone gives to Ivy,
Ivy gives the best gift of all.

For Baba

All rights reserved. Published by Arthur A. Levine Books, an imprint of Scholastic Inc., *Publishers since 1920*, by arrangement with Little Hare Books, Surry Hills, Australia. SCHOLASTIC and the LANTERN LOGO are trademarks and/or registered trademarks of Scholastic Inc.

Library of Congress Cataloging-in-Publication Data

Blackwood, Freya.
Ivy loves to give / Freya Blackwood. — 1st American ed.
p. cm.
Summary: Ivy loves to give presents, and although they are not always appropriate,
they are always given with enthusiasm and generosity.
ISBN 978-0-545-23467-2 (hardcover : alk. paper) [1. Gifts—Fiction. 2. Generosity—Fiction. 3. Humorous stories.] I. Title.
PZ7.B53376Iv 2010
[E] —dc22
2009042156

The art for this book was created using pencil and watercolor.

10 9 8 7 6 5 4 3 2 1   10 11 12 13 14

Printed in China

First American edition, September 2010

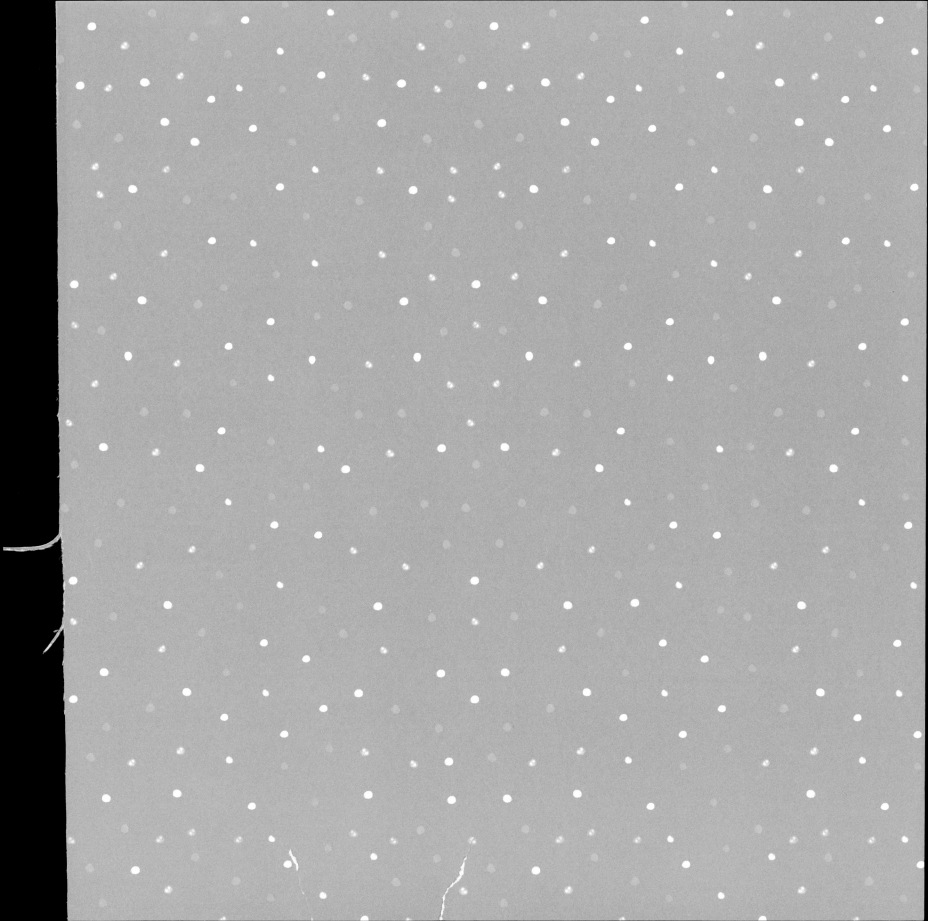